A Beginning-to-Read Book

Astro the Alien Visits Forest Animals

by Emily Sohn

Illustrated by Carlos Aón

NORWOOD HOUSE PRESS

DEAR CAREGIVER,

Books in the Beginning-to-Read collection are carefully written to develop the skills of early readers. The *Astro the Alien* series is a step up from the introductory *Dear Dragon* series. It provides early readers the opportunity to learn about the world through the narrative while building on their previous reading skills. The text in these books is comprised of common sight words and content words to expand your child's vocabulary. Increasing readers' sight word recognition promotes their reading fluency. The vivid pictures are an opportunity for readers to interact with the text and increase their understanding.

Begin by reading the story as your child follows along. Then let your child read familiar words. As your child practices with the text, you will notice improved accuracy, rate, and expression until he or she is able to read the story independently. Praising your child's efforts will build his or her confidence as an independent reader. Discussing the pictures will help your child make connections between the story and his or her own life. Reinforce literacy using the activities at the back of the book to support your child's reading comprehension, reading fluency, and oral language skills.

Above all, encourage your child to have fun with the reading experience!

Marla Conn, MS, Ed., Literacy Consultant

Norwood House Press • P.O. Box 316598 • Chicago, Illinois 60631

For more information about Norwood House Press please visit our website at www.norwoodhousepress.com or call 866-565-2900.

© 2019 Norwood House Press. Beginning-to-Read™ is a trademark of Norwood House Press.

Library of Congress Cataloging-in-Publication Data

Names: Sohn, Emily, author.
Title: Astro the Alien visits forest animals / by Emily Sohn.
Description: Chicago, Illinois : Norwood House Press, [2018] | Series: Beginning-to-read | Summary: "Astro the Alien and his friends Ben and Eva visit and learn about forest animals, including deer, raccoons, and squirrels. Includes reading activities and a word list"-- Provided by publisher.
Identifiers: LCCN 2018005660 (print) | LCCN 2018013282 (ebook) | ISBN 9781684041916 (pdf) | ISBN 9781599539195 (hardcover : alk. paper) | ISBN 9781684041848 (pbk. : alk. paper)
Subjects: | CYAC: Forest animals--Fiction. | Extraterrestrial beings--Fiction.
Classification: LCC PZ7.1.S662 (ebook) | LCC PZ7.1.S662 Asr 2018 (print) | DDC [E]--dc23
LC record available at https://lccn.loc.gov/2018005660

Hardcover ISBN: 978-1-59953-919-5   Paperback ISBN: 978-1-68404-184-8
312N—072018
Manufactured in the United States of America in North Mankato, Minnesota.

"One, two, three," said Ben.
"Ready or not, here I come!"

"It would be fun to play this in a forest," said Ben.

"We could hide in the trees," said Eva. "We might meet some forest animals."

"We can go in my space pod," said Astro.

They got in the pod and took off. Soon they landed in a forest.

"Ready or not, here I come!"
said Eva. "I see wood mice.
Those are rodents. But where
are Ben and Astro?"

Eva saw something move.
She heard a noise.

"Ben?" said Eva. "Astro?"

"That is a deer!" said Eva.
"It has antlers. It is a buck."

"That is a doe. It has no antlers."

"There is a raccoon," said Ben.
"They usually come out at night."

"That one must be going home to bed," said Astro.

"A skunk!" said Eva. "Stinky! I do not want to get sprayed."

"I will stay far from the black bear!" said Eva. "I hope Ben and Astro are not too close."

"We should split up, Astro," said Ben. "We will be harder to find."

"Yes," said Astro. "I'll go that way."

"Eva will never find me up here," said Ben. "But I found some squirrels. They are good climbers."

"A woodpecker," said Ben.
"They drill holes in trees.
They find bugs to eat."

"This owl sleeps during the day. It hunts at night."

"That is a slug," said Astro. "It looks slimy. And that is a snake. It looks slithery. I think I will hide somewhere else."

"There is a fox," said Eva. "It has good hearing. I wonder if it hears Ben and Astro?"

"The badger digs holes. Are Ben and Astro hiding underground?"

"I found you!" said Eva.

"Have you found Astro yet?" asked Ben.

"No," said Eva. "Let's go find him."

"Here he is!" Eva said. "We had a busy day in the forest."

"Let's wake him up and go home," Ben said.

"We saw a lot of animals in the forest today," Eva said.

"You are good at finding things, Eva!" said Astro and Ben.

Comprehension Strategy

To check your child's understanding of the book, recreate the following cause and effect diagram on a sheet of paper. After your child reads the book, ask him or her to fill in the empty boxes with the cause or effect that is missing.

CAUSE	EFFECT
Astro, Ben, and Eva want to play hide-and-seek.	
	Eva runs away from the skunk.
Astro and Ben want to be harder for Eva to find.	

Vocabulary Lesson

Content words are words that are specific to a particular topic. All of the content words for this book can be found on page 32. Use some or all of these content words to complete one or more of the following activities:

- Ask your child to find content words that refer to foods animals eat.
- Have your child pick out content words for animals they would or would not like to get close to.
- Challenge your child to find content words that are categories for kinds of animals.
- Use content words to describe an animal. Have your child name the animal and imitate it. Switch roles.
- Pick 10 content words and write each word or draw a picture of it on two pieces of paper. Turn the 20 pieces of paper upside down and place them in a grid. Turning just two over at a time, see if you can use your memory to match all 10 words as fast as possible.

Close Reading

Close reading helps children comprehend text. It includes reading a text, discussing it with others, and answering questions about it. Use these questions to discuss this book with your child:

- Do you think it would be fun to play hide-and-seek in a forest? Why or why not?
- Why didn't Eva want to upset the skunk?
- Have you ever been to a forest or seen one on TV? What kinds of animals did you see there?
- How can you tell the difference between a male and a female deer?
- Play a game of hide-and-seek. Each round, have every player who is hiding pretend to be one of the animals in the book. Can you find them all?

Foundational Skills

A pronoun replaces a noun in a sentence. Have your child identify the words that are pronouns in the list below. Then help your child find pronouns in this book.

she	a	bear	he	and	I
Astro	it	close	slug	are	they

Fluency

Fluency is the ability to read accurately with speed and expression. Help your child practice fluency by using one or more of the following activities:

- Reread this book to your child at least two times while he or she uses a finger to track each word as you read it.
- Read the first sentence aloud. Then have your child reread the sentence with you. Continue until you have finished this book.
- Ask your child to read aloud the words they know on each page of this book. (Your child will learn additional words with subsequent readings.)
- Have your child practice reading this book several times to improve accuracy, rate, and expression.

WORD LIST

Astro the Alien uses the 145 words listed below. The words bolded below serve as an introduction to new vocabulary, while the unbolded words are more familiar or frequently used. You may wish to write the words on index cards and use them to help your child build automatic word recognition. Regular practice with these words will enhance your child's fluency in reading connected text.

a	can	found	him	**might**	**raccoon**	**sprayed**	**underground**
and	**climbers**	fox	holes	move	**ready**	**squirrels**	up
animals	close	from	home	**must**	**rodents**	**stay**	**usually**
antlers	come	fun	hope	my		**stinky**	
are	could		**hunts**		said		**wake**
asked		get		never	saw	that	want
Astro	day	go(ing)	I	**night**	see	the	way
at	deer	good	**I'll**	no	she	there	we
	digs	got	if	**noise**	**should**	they	**where**
badger	do	had	in	not	skunk	things	will
be	**doe**	harder	is	of	sleeps	**think**	**wonder**
bear	**drill**	has	it	off	**slimy**	this	wood
bed	**during**	have		one	**slithery**	those	**woodpecker**
Ben		he	**landed**	or	**slug**	three	**would**
black	eat	heard	let's	out	**snake**	to	
buck	**else**	hearing	looks	owl	some	today	yes
bugs	Eva	hears	lot		**something**	too	**yet**
busy		here		play	**somewhere**	took	you
but	**far**	**hide**	me	**pod**	soon	trees	
	find(ing)	**hiding**	meet		**space**	two	
	forest		mice		**split**		

ABOUT THE AUTHOR

Emily Sohn is an award-winning journalist in Minneapolis, Minnesota. She writes for many magazines and newspapers and has written dozens of graphic novels and other books for kids. She started her career as the science writer on an expedition team that produced interactive, educational content for a website that was viewed by hundreds of thousands of students in classrooms around the world.

ABOUT THE ILLUSTRATOR

Carlos Aón was born in Buenos Aires, Argentina. He studied in a comic book art academy for four years. In 2000, he graduated as a graphic designer. Aón's work appears in dozens of graphic novels, story books, and educational projects in the United States, Argentina, Europe, and Asia.

32